Dear Parent:
Your child's love of reading starts here!

Every child learns to read in a different way and at his or her own speed. You can help your young reader improve and become more confident by encouraging his or her own interests and abilities. You can also guide your child's spiritual development by reading stories with biblical values and Bible stories, like I Can Read! books published by Zonderkidz. From books your child reads with you to the first books he or she reads alone, there are I Can Read! books for every stage of reading:

SHARED READING
Basic language, word repetition, and whimsical illustrations, ideal for sharing with your emergent reader.

BEGINNING READING
Short sentences, familiar words, and simple concepts for children eager to read on their own.

READING WITH HELP
Engaging stories, longer sentences, and language play for developing readers.

READING ALONE
Complex plots, challenging vocabulary, and high-interest topics for the independent reader.

ADVANCED READING
Short paragraphs, chapters, and exciting themes for the perfect bridge to chapter books.

I Can Read! books have introduced children to the joy of reading since 1957. Featuring award-winning authors and illustrators and a fabulous cast of beloved characters, I Can Read! books set the standard for beginning readers.

A lifetime of discovery begins with the magical words **"I Can Read!"**

Visit www.icanread.com for information on enriching your child's reading experience.
Visit www.zonderkidz.com for more Zonderkidz I Can Read! titles.

Be kind and compassionate
to one another.
—Ephesians 4:32

ZONDERKIDZ

The Princess Twins and the Birthday Party
Copyright © 2011 by Zonderkidz

Requests for information should be addressed to:

Zonderkidz, *Grand Rapids, Michigan 49530*

Library of Congress Cataloging-in-Publication Data

Hodgson, Mona Gansber, 1954–
    The princess twins and the birthday party / by Mona Hodgson.
       p. cm. — (I can read!)
    Summary: After spending hours preparing for their birthday party, the twin princesses Abby and Emma
learn that outward appearances should only be a reflection of inner beauty.
       ISBN 978-0-310-72707-1 (softcover)
    [1. Princesses—Fiction. 2. Birthdays—Fiction. 3. Twins—Fiction. 4. Sisters—Fiction. 5. Kindness—Fiction
6. Christian life—Fiction.] I. Title
PZ7.H6649Pr 2012
    [E]—dc22   2010052438

Editor: Mary Hassinger
Art direction & design: Sarah Molegraaf

Printed in China

12 13 14 15 16 17 /DSC/ 7 6 5 4 3 2 1

Story by Mona Hodgson
Pictures by Red Hansen

Princess Emma's eyes popped open.

Emma jumped out of bed.

"Today is our birthday!"

Princess Abby jumped up.

"Happy Birthday, Emma."

Emma hugged her twin sister.

"Happy Birthday to you too."

The princesses picked out
their prettiest dresses.

Emma and Abby pinned up their hair.

They put pretty crowns
on their heads.

"We're ready for our special day,"
said Princess Emma.

Princess Emma and Princess Abby

walked down the stairs.

Emma and Abby ate pancakes
and drank apple juice.

"It's almost time for our party,"
Emma said.

Emma twirled.

"You look beautiful," said the queen.

"You are even more beautiful inside.

God sees your heart," said the king.

"He sees you are loving and kind."

Later Emma and Abby
made pretty name cards.

They put them next to the tea cups.

There was a place for each friend.

The castle bell rang.

The princesses ran to the door.

They said hello to each girl.

Emma looked at her friends,

but she didn't see Beth.

"Where's Beth?" she asked.

"She left," said one of the girls.

Emma looked outside.

She saw Beth down the path.

"Beth, wait," said Emma.

She ran to catch up with her friend.

"What's wrong?" asked Emma.

"My dress is too plain," Beth said.

Emma didn't want Beth

to miss the party.

"I know what you need," said Emma.

She took the crown off her head.

Emma set the crown on Beth's head.

Beth twirled.

"I feel beautiful," she said.

"Thank you for your kindness."

"You are beautiful," said Emma.

"And you are even more beautiful inside."

The girls ran back to the party.